MARVEL WEST S...

THE AVENGERS

» AVENGERS: ASSEMBLE!

Written by
Tomas Palacios

Based on Marvel's
The Avengers
Motion Picture Written by
Joss Whedon

Illustrated by
Lee Garbett,
John Lucas, and
Lee Duhig

Based on
Marvel Comics'
The Avengers

MARVEL
NEW YORK

marvelkids.com

Printed in the United States of America
First Edition
3 5 7 9 10 8 6 4
G658-7729A-12202
ISBN 978-1-4231-5481-5

This is the story of the Avengers!

Meet Tony Stark.

He is very smart.

He likes to build things.

Tony built a suit of armor.

He is now called Iron Man!

Iron Man can fly!

This is Bruce Banner.

He is a scientist.

He works in a lab.

When Bruce gets angry,

he turns into the Hulk!

The Hulk is very big

and green!

Next is Thor.

He is from another world.

Thor has a magical hammer.

He can control lightning!

Thor has a brother.

His name is Loki.

Loki is a very sneaky villain.

Steve Rogers is small and weak.

He wants to be big and strong.

He wants to fight
for what is right.

Later, he becomes

Captain America!

He fights for justice!

Cap has a shield.

It is red, white, and blue.

Next up is Clint Barton.

His code name is Hawkeye.

He uses a bow and arrow.

He is a great shot!

There is also

Natasha Romanoff.

She is called Black Widow.

She is a superspy

and a good fighter!

Finally, there is Nick Fury.

He is the leader of S.H.I.E.L.D.

S.H.I.E.L.D. is a special

group that helps people.

Nick Fury wants to make

a new group to assist

S.H.I.E.L.D.

Nick Fury creates

a team of Super Heroes.

He calls them the Avengers!

The Avengers fight for good.

They use their powers

to stop bad guys.

When there is trouble,

the Avengers assemble!